MW01070593

SIMON SPOTLIGHT
An imprint of Simon & Schuster Children's Publishing Division
1230 Avenue of the Americas
New York, New York 10020

Designed and produced by Les Livres du Dragon d'Or

Adapted from the animated television series *The Busy World of Richard Scarry,*
produced by Paramount Pictures Corporation and Cinar.

Manufactured in Italy
First Edition
10 9 8 7 6 5 4 3 2 1
ISBN 0-689-81650-2

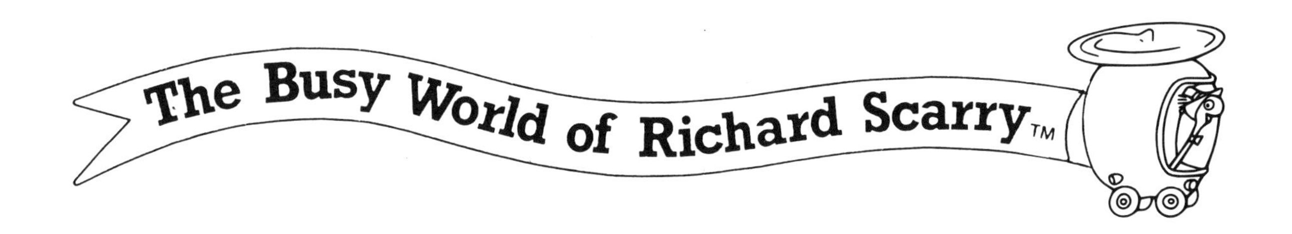

Richard Scarry's

BEST HISTORY OF THE WORLD EVER!

SIMON SPOTLIGHT

Table of Contents

THE FIRST PYRAMID

Welcome to Egypt!
This ancient land is famous for its great pyramids. These huge stone monuments are where the pharaohs, the kings of Egypt, are buried.
The first pyramid was built by the pharaoh's architect, Imhotep—with a little help from his son, Twomotep.

Their story takes place nearly five thousand years ago, in the reign of Pharaoh Zoser.
Imhotep has been summoned by the pharaoh.
"You may rise, Imhotep," says the pharaoh, "I have wonderful news for you!"

“I would like you to build the most magnificent monument ever!” Pharaoh Zoser tells Imhotep.

“I am honored,” Imhotep replies. “I only hope that I can design such a thing.”

In his studio Imhotep sets quickly to work.
Just then his son Twomotep enters. “Would you like to go fishing with me, Father?”

“Not now, Son,” replies Imhotep. “First I have to finish my drawings for the pharaoh.”
“But you *always* have to finish your drawings first,” says Twomotep sadly.

"Have a look at my plan,"
Imhotep says.
"Wow! It's amazing!"
says Twomotep.

"I am going to show my idea
to the pharaoh right away,"
says Imhotep. "I hope he will
like it."

Imhotep runs to the pharaoh.
"Good luck, father!" Twomotep calls
after him. While his father is gone,
the young boy tries to build his
father's monument with his toy blocks.

Twomotep gently places the last block on his little monument. It begins to wobble and shake. Uh-oh!

Crash! The blocks fall down. "Oh, no!" exclaims Twomotep. "What if this happens to Father's real monument?"

"I must warn him at once!" Twomotep says. He runs to the construction site.

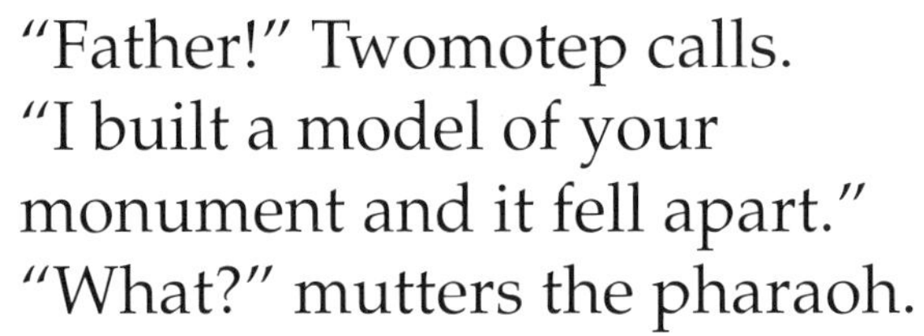

"Father!" Twomotep calls.
"I built a model of your
monument and it fell apart."
"What?" mutters the pharaoh.

"It is unwise to joke like that in
front of the pharaoh, my son,"
Imhotep warns.
"But it's true!" Twomotep says.

Suddenly they hear a big roar: *Boom! Bang! Crash!*
Imhotep's monument is falling down! Watch out everyone!

“This is a disaster!” Imhotep exclaims.

Pharaoh Zoser is furious. “You have until midnight to design a proper monument or you’ll go to jail,” he warns Imhotep.

Back in his studio, Imhotep tries desperately to find another idea.
An angry guard is watching.
Hurry, Imhotep, time is running out!
Just then a gust of wind blows Imhotep’s plan onto the floor.

Swoosh! The plan lands upside down at Imhotep’s feet. Imhotep looks at it. “Hey! That gives me an idea!” he says. “Twomotep, bring your blocks. We’re going to see the pharaoh right away!”

"If we build the same monument upside down, it will be perfectly balanced," Imhotep explains to the pharaoh. "See?" He shows Pharaoh Zoser the blocks. "I call it a pyramid!" says Imhotep.

"Good work, Imhotep and Twomotep!" congratulates Pharaoh Zoser. "As a reward, you may have anything you like!" "I'd like to have more time with my father," says Twomotep.

"Well, as soon as the pyramid is finished, I promise to grant your wish, Twomotep," Pharaoh Zoser says.

From the hieroglyphs carved on the pyramid, it looks like little Twomotep got his wish!

Nowadays you can still admire Imhotep's wonderful pyramid!

THE FIRST VALENTINE

Every February 14 we celebrate Valentine's Day. It is an ancient tradition, which may have started back in imperial Rome . . .

Givius is the secretary to the Roman emperor. He is also secretly in love with the emperor's daughter, Valentina. He and his assistant, Maximius, are bringing the emperor his important papers. Please don't run in the halls, Givius!

Whoops!
Givius bumps into Valentina. The emperor's papers tumble to the floor. Good going, Givius!

"Um, please excuse me, I'm sorry," Givius apologizes. "It's all right," replies Valentina. "Let me help you."

"Thank you, Vatenlina . . .
I mean, Valentina," mumbles
Givius.

"Hello, Givius!" says the emperor.
"Is everything all right?"

"No . . . I mean, yes," Givius
mumbles.
"Excellent," says the emperor.
"Then you may go."
Givius and Maximius return to
their office.

"Isn't Givius cute, Father?"
Valentina says.
"If you think so, Daughter,"
replies the emperor.

Later Givius and Maximius relax at the imperial steam baths. The emperor is there also, but because of the steam, the two boys do not see him. "What will I do, Maximius?" asks Givius, "I'm in love with Valentina but I'm too shy to tell her."

The emperor overhears this. He gets an idea and hides behind a statue.

"Givius!" shouts the emperor, with a deep voice.
"Maximius! The statue is talking!" whispers Givius, amazed.

"Givius!" the emperor booms, "If you love someone, do not be afraid to show your true colors!"
"How can I show Valentina my feelings?" wonders Givius.
"Maybe you could give her a gift," Maximius suggests.
The two boys leave the baths.

Good work, Emperor!

Givius has an idea.
Just outside Valentina's window, Givius and Maximius decorate a bare winter tree. Then Givius tosses a pebble at the window to attract Valentina's attention.

"Look, Father!" Valentina exclaims. "What a lovely surprise!"

"Ouch!" yells the emperor. "Who dares throw stones at their emperor?"

"Guards!" the emperor calls. "Find Givius and bring him to me at once!"
"Uh-oh," Givius mutters, "I think we're in trouble."

"We'd better leave the palace before the guards catch us!" Maximius suggests.
"We're on our way," Givius replies, "but first I have to leave a special note for Valentina."
On tiptoes they approach Valentina's room.

"Not so fast, boys!" calls a guard, jumping out from behind a pillar. He brings them to the emperor.

"Now, Givius," says the emperor, "was it *you* who decorated my daughter's garden and also bonked me on the head with a pebble?"
"Yes, sir," Givius replies. "I'm sorry, it was an accident."

"Then why did you write this card for my daughter, saying 'I Love You'?" asks the emperor.

"Remember the voice in the baths!" Maximius whispers to Givius. "Show your true colors!"

Givius hesitates, then bravely tells the emperor the truth.
"I wrote this note because I'm in love with Valentina!" he declares.
"Then you must give it to her, Givius," says the emperor. "I think she loves you too!"

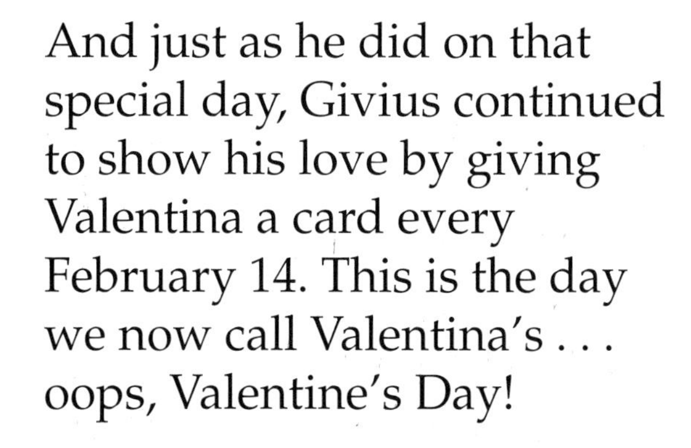

And just as he did on that special day, Givius continued to show his love by giving Valentina a card every February 14. This is the day we now call Valentina's . . . oops, Valentine's Day!

P. J. PIG'S BRAVE DAY

Once upon a time, way back in history, a young squire named P. J. Pig wanted to wear a shining suit of armor and be a brave knight. It was his biggest dream.

P. J. is playing at being a brave knight.

Suddenly he finds three *real* knights—all tied up!

P. J. quickly unties them.
"What happened to you?" P. J. asks the knights.
"A scary dragon tied us up and kidnapped Princess Lily," they reply.

“Then let’s go after them!” P. J. tells the knights. “We must save Princess Lily!”
“You can’t expect us to chase a fierce dragon without our speedy mounts and a hearty dinner,” says the first knight.
“Besides, it’s getting dark,” the second knight adds.
“Come on, be brave!” says P. J. “You are knights, aren’t you?”

By the time they reach the dragon’s lair, it is night.
“After a good night’s sleep, we’ll be ready to attack the dragon,” P. J says.
“If only we *could* sleep,” complain the knights. “These suits of armor are so uncomfortable.”

"Wait, I've got an idea!" P. J. exclaims.

"What if we turn these banners into sleeping clothes?" he suggests. In no time P. J. has cut up the banners. What a good idea, P. J.!

"Thank you, P. J.!" exclaim the three knights. "These sleeping clothes are wonderfully light and comfortable. Bravo and good night!"
"Good night!" replies P. J.

Thanks to P. J.'s sleeping clothes, the knights sleep like babies! The next day they are ready to attack.
"Be quiet!" P. J. commands as they enter the dragon's cave.

"It's the dragon!" exclaim the knights.
"Hmm . . . I think there is something funny about this dragon," P. J. whispers.
"Ha, ha! It's just a disguise!" he says. "That gives me another idea. . . ."

Indeed, four ruffians have kidnapped Princess Lily, using the dragon disguise. But why do they look so frightened?

Roaarr!
"A dragon!" shout the ruffians.
"Quick, we must hide!"

"Come inside the cell," Princess Lily tells the ruffians. "You'll be safe in here!"

The four ruffians enter the cell.
Faster than you can say "dragon," Princess Lily grabs the key, runs out the door, and locks it behind her.
"How clever you are, Princess Lily!" the knights say.
"Thank you, boys!" she tells P. J. and the knights. "Using the dragon costume was a good idea too."

Back at the castle, the knights tell the king about their adventure and P. J.'s wonderful sleeping clothes. To honor the invention, the king decides to name these new clothes after their inventor.
"What is your name, young squire?" the king asks.
"Pajamas Pig, your Majesty," replies P. J. "But everyone just calls me P. J."

And that's not all! To thank P. J. for rescuing Princess Lily, the King makes P. J. a knight and gives him a suit of shining armor.

P. J. is thrilled!
His dream has finally come true!
And today, when you and I dream, we wear our pj's!

MARTHA'S FIRST BOOK

Did you know that a long time ago not many people could read? That is because there were not many books. Each book had to be written by hand, and so it took a long time to make them. But one day in Germany, an inventor named Herr Gutenbear changed all that—thanks to the visit of a little girl named Martha.

"*Guten Tag*, Herr Gutenbear!" says Martha, knocking at Herr Gutenbear's door. "I would like to learn to read. I have heard that you have some books. Can you please teach me?" she asks.

"Certainly!" replies Herr Gutenbear. "Just as soon as I finish my latest invention, the laundry press!"

"Maybe when you finish your laundry press, you could invent something to make books," Martha suggests.

"What a good idea, Martha!" Herr Gutenbear exclaims. "I think I know a way to do it."

Herr Gutenbear dips his paw into an inkwell. *Splash!* "What are you doing?" asks Martha.

"Look at the pawprints," Herr Gutenbear tells Martha. "Maybe I can also print letters by taking alphabet blocks and dipping them into ink."

"When pressed onto paper, the letters will make words, and words will make sentences, and sentences will fill pages to make books!" Herr Gutenbear explains. "My, that would be wonderful!" Martha exclaims.

"Come back tomorrow," Herr Gutenbear tells Martha. "By then my new invention should be ready!"

The next day Martha hurries to Herr Gutenbear's house.

Herr Gutenbear's house is a mess!
"Are you all right, Herr Gutenbear?" asks Martha.
"Ach, yes!" replies Herr Gutenbear. "It's my machine which is having some trouble."

"You see, I can't get it to press the laundry *and* print the alphabet letters too," he explains.

"Maybe you could make *two* different machines, one that prints books and one that presses laundry," suggests Martha.

“You are a genius, Martha!” Herr Gutenbear says. “Thank you!” Herr Gutenbear removes the clothes wringers from the machine.

He puts the carved alphabet blocks in their place.

“Are you ready to print, Martha?” Herr Gutenbear asks.
“Ready, Captain!” she answers.

Herr Gutenbear puts a piece of paper on a board and lowers the press with the inky letters. *Cling! Clang! Boom!*

When he raises the press again, he is amazed.
"It's working! It's printed!" Herr Gutenbear exclaims. He takes the paper out of the press.

"This is the very first page of a book I'm printing especially for you, Martha!" Herr Gutenbear says.

"Wow! My very own book!" exclaims Martha. "Oh, thank you, Herr Gutenbear!"

"But I will need an assistant to finish this first book," says Herr Gutenbear.

"Perhaps you would like to work with me?" he asks Martha.
"Of course I would!" says Martha.

As you can imagine, by helping Herr Gutenbear to print books, Martha learned to read in no time. So did her friends, and people in other towns too! Thanks to Herr Gutenbear's printing press, everyone has books at home. Thank you, Herr Gutenbear!

MACARONI POLO

Some nine hundred years ago, the young explorer Marco Polo and his father Niccolo set out on a trip from Venice, Italy, to China. It was a very long journey by ship across stormy seas and then by foot across hot deserts.
But few people know that Marco brought along his little brother Macaroni to cook their meals.

After months of traveling, the three explorers arrive at the palace of Kublai Khan, the great emperor of China. Isn't it impressive!

The emperor receives Marco, Niccolo, and Macaroni in the throne room.
I'm not sure that he is pleased to see them!
"Come forward!" Kublai Khan orders.

Macaroni sees a beautiful vase nearby.

Be careful, Macaroni!
It's not a toy!

Boom! Crash!
Oops! I think you're in trouble, Macaroni!

Kublai Khan is furious. "Guards!" he calls. "Take the Polo family away, and do not let them leave my court!"

Macaroni, Marco, and Niccolo have to sit and wait until Kublai Khan forgets the incident.

They wait the whole afternoon. Macaroni is getting hungry! "I'm going to the kitchen," he says. "No more accidents, please, Macaroni!" warns his brother.

In the kitchen the cooks are busy preparing the emperor's dinner.
"What are you cooking?" asks Macaroni.

"Something new!" replies the head cook. "Hot soup with dough balls."

Macaroni tries to taste a dough ball but it rolls off his chopstick . . . and lands in a sieve. *Plop!*
The dough ball unravels and goes through the holes of the sieve, turning into curly strings.
"This is funny!" Macaroni says.

Meanwhile the head cook brings his meal to the emperor.

Kublai Khan tries to pick up a dough ball with his chopsticks.

Zip! The ball rolls off the sticks and falls back into the soup.
Splash! The emperor's gown is splattered with soup.
"What a mess!" he growls.

"Bring me something I can eat!" the emperor shouts to the head cook. "And be quick—I am very hungry!" My, the emperor doesn't sound very nice, does he?

The head cook doesn’t know what to do. “I have an idea!” Macaroni says. “If we make the dough balls smaller, they will be easier to eat.”

Macaroni takes the dough strings from the sieve and cuts them into small pieces. Good idea, Macaroni!

This time Kublai Khan has no trouble picking up the food.

Still, Macaroni and the head cook hope that he *likes* it too!

"Yum! This is delicious!" Kublai Khan finally smiles. "Who made it?" "Macaroni did," replies the head cook.

"Well done, Macaroni!" says Kublai Khan. "Such a good cook deserves a special reward!"

The emperor gives many splendid gifts to the three explorers. When Marco, Niccolo, and Macaroni return to Venice, they prepare the emperor's new meal for Mrs. Polo. And can you guess what they call it? Why, macaroni, of course!

DONA FELIPA AND AMERIGO DISCOVER AMERICA

Do you know who discovered America? Christopher Columoose! The whole story started some five hundred years ago in Palos, Spain. At that time people believed that the earth was flat. But Christopher Columoose thought the earth was as round as an apple. One day he decided to sail to the Orient, which is *east* of Spain. To prove the earth was round, he sailed toward the *west*.

Dona Felipa and Amerigo want to be a part of the trip too! Quick, jump in this basket! It's about to be carried on board the ship.

"Umpf! This is heavy!"

Soon the Nina, the Pinta, and the Santa Maria are ready to begin their adventurous journey westward.

That evening Columoose praises his first mate, Alonzo. "You and the crew are brave to sail where no one has sailed before!"

When it is night, Dona Felipa and Amerigo sneak out of the basket and climb on deck.
"This is beautiful!" Dona Felipa gasps, as she looks up at the starry sky.
Uh-oh! Someone is coming!

"Aha! A stowaway!" Alonzo exclaims, as he picks up Dona Felipa.
Luckily, he doesn't see Amerigo.

"Stowaways are to be clapped in irons," says Alonzo. "We'll take care of you later."

Poor Dona Felipa!
"I knew we shouldn't have come on this trip!" groans Amerigo.

Suddenly they hear footsteps.
Amerigo quickly hides.
The crewmen enter the cabin, and they don't seem happy.

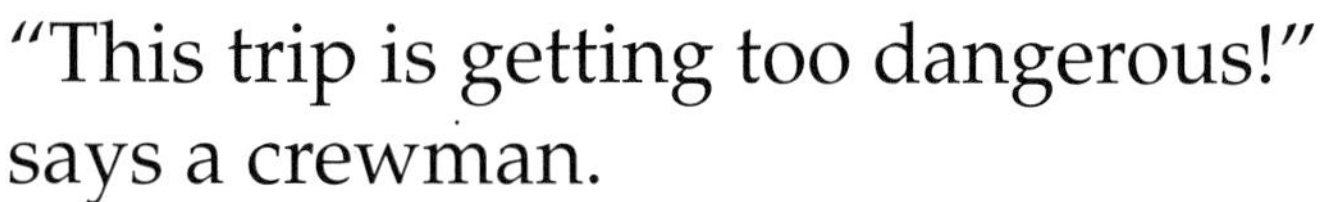

“This trip is getting too dangerous!” says a crewman.
“I bet we’re lost!” says another.
“We must turn back to Spain before it’s too late!”

“Admiral Columoose is in danger, Amerigo,” Dona Felipa whispers. “You *must* help him!”

Amerigo runs to warn Columoose. Just then a large piece of paper falls through a crack in the ceiling. It lands on Amerigo. *Oof!*
“Hey! This looks like a map!” he says.

The angry crewmen tell Columoose to turn his ship around.

"Don't worry," says Columoose, "we're not lost at all! I'll show you where we are on the map."

What map, Columoose?

"*This* map!" says Amerigo. He pulls it up through the floorboards.

"Thank you very much," says Columoose. "But who are you?"
"I'm Amerigo and I'm here with my wife, Dona Felipa. We are . . . stowaways," he replies.
"As you've been very helpful, you're now part of the crew!" decides Columoose.

"Look," says Columoose,
"here's exactly where we are."
He points to a spot on the map.
"I promise you we'll find land
very soon!"
"Can you please also release
Dona Felipa very soon?" asks
Amerigo.
"Of course," says Columoose.

Thanks to Amerigo,
Columoose found his
map. The crew helped
the ship sail safely to a
new land, which today
we call America.

Hmm . . . I wonder
where *that* name comes from?

THE BEST PAINTER EVER

Buon giorno! This story takes place at the Vatican in Rome, some four hundred years ago, during a time called the Renaissance. There were many great artists then, but no one greater than Michael Antelope.

Padre Giovanni comes to see Michael Antelope with a special request from the Pope. "The Pope would like you to paint the walls of the Sistine Chapel!" he tells Michael. "What an honor!" exclaims Michael. "Let's go take a look at it!"

"This is such a beautiful chapel!" says Michael. "Did you bring along all my paints, Antonio?" he asks his assistant.
"Yes, Maestro," replies Antonio.
"Then let's begin!" decides Michael.

"Can you play something lively while I paint?" Michael asks his assistant.
"Yes, Maestro," replies Antonio, and he begins to play on his pan flute.
Tweet! Toot! Tweet!

Michael Antelope is soon finished with his first painting.
"Thank you for the music, Antonio!" he says. "How do you like my work?"
"It's truly beautiful!" Antonio praises.

Knock! Knock!
It's Padre Giovanni!
"Hello, Michael and Antonio!" he says.
"Can I take a look at your painting?"

"Go ahead, Padre,"
replies Michael.
"We're going to have
lunch now. Ciao!"

"My, what a wonderful painting!" Padre Giovanni says.
"Michael really is a genius! The Pope will be so pleased!"

"Why, this olive tree looks so real, I could pick an olive right off it," says Padre Giovanni.
Watch out, Padre Giovanni, it's fresh paint! *Whoops!*

Padre Giovanni has smudged Michael Antelope's painting.
He tries to clean the smudge with his robe. *Swoosh! Swoosh!*
But he erases the whole tree instead.
Mamma mia! What a mess!

After a tasty lunch, Michael and Antonio return to the chapel to continue their work. Little do they know what Padre Giovanni has done to the painting!

Padre Giovanni meets them at the chapel door.
"I'm sorry, Michael," says Padre Giovanni. "I seem to have smudged your painting. It may need just a little touch-up."

"A little touch-up!" grumbles Michael.
He rushes over to his painting.
Padre Giovanni has erased everything!
"This is a disaster!" shouts Michael.
"I have to do my work all over again!"
Poor Michael Antelope!

"I've got to find a way to prevent Padre Giovanni from ruining my work," Michael thinks. "What if . . ."

A few days later, Padre Giovanni brings Cardinal Lion to see the painted walls of the chapel.

But instead of being pleased, Cardinal Lion is furious. The walls are empty! "Where are the paintings?" he demands.

"If this is a joke, I don't find it funny, Padre Giovanni," Cardinal Lion mutters.

"Yoo-hoo!" calls a voice from above. It's Michael Antelope! To protect his paintings from Padre Giovanni, he has painted on the *ceiling* instead!

"It's beautiful!" cries Cardinal Lion.

"You really are the best painter ever!" shouts Padre Giovanni.

He is right!

Even today, tourists from all over the world come to Rome to admire Michael Antelope's masterpiece in the Sistine Chapel.

Bravo, Michael!

PIGGY ORIGAMI

This story takes place a long time ago in a small village in Japan. Piggy Origami's granddaughter is getting married today. He wants the wedding to be perfect!

Everyone in the village is busy preparing for the wedding. Piggy Origami wants to help too.

He tries to unload a bag of rice.
Watch out, Origami!
It's heavy!

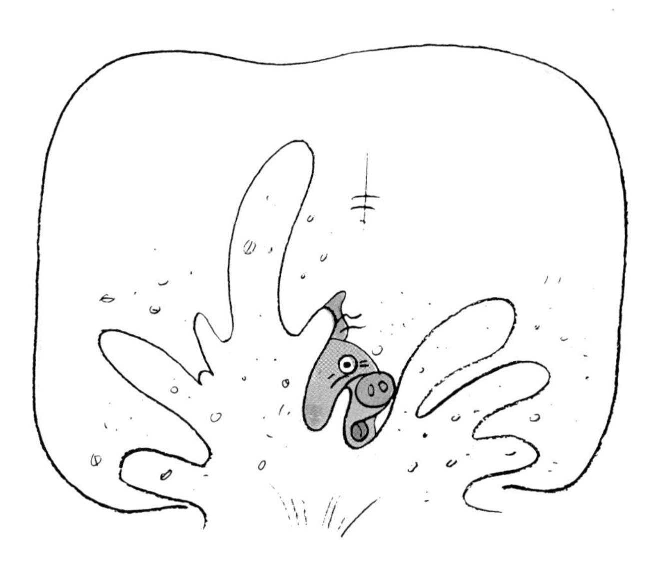

Umpf! Boom!

What a mess! There is rice everywhere! Are you all right, Origami?

"These rice bags are too heavy for you, Origami," says a villager. "Maybe someone else needs your help with something easier."

Nearby, Origami finds his granddaughter decorating the garden with candles.
"Maybe I can help her," he thinks.

But when he gets closer, Origami sees that she is weeping.
"Why are you crying, Granddaughter?" he asks.
"I wish the garden to be filled with flowers for my wedding," she replies.

"Do not cry anymore, Granddaughter," says Origami. "I think I can help!"

Origami sets off quickly for Lord Kyushu's palace.
"I will ask Lord Kyushu for flowers and ornaments," Origami says.

"I am here to see Lord Kyushu!"
Origami tells the palace guard.

"Do you have an appointment?"
the guard demands.

“I’m afraid I don’t,” replies Origami.
“No appointment, no audience!”
says the guard. “I’m sorry.”
Origami sadly turns to leave, when
he sees a pile of palace garbage.

There are many
colored papers
among the garbage.
“May I take the
papers?” Origami
asks the guard.
“Help yourself!”
the guard replies.

“What are you going to do with them?”
asks the guard.
“I’m going to give my granddaughter
the best wedding present ever!”
Origami tells him.

Back at home Origami sets quickly to work. He cuts and folds the papers, giving each one a different shape. Soon he turns the garden into a colorful paper wonderland! Hurry, Origami! The party is about to begin.

"What a beautiful garden!" his granddaughter exclaims. "Who did such a marvelous thing?"

"I did, Granddaughter," says Origami. "Happy wedding!" "Oh, this is the best wedding present I could ever hope for!" she says.

From his palace Lord Kyushu sees the beautiful garden through his telescope.

Lord Kyushu is amazed! He decides to inspect the garden himself.

"Bravo, Origami!" says Lord Kyushu, picking up a flower. "These are marvelous paper creations!"
"Sir, that flower is real," whispers the guard.

"What do you call your folded paper creations?" asks Lord Kyushu.
"Um, I don't know," replies Piggy Origami.
"Then we will name them after *you*!" says Lord Kyushu.
And since that day, the art of paper folding—origami—has been a popular tradition. Thank you, Piggy Origami!